Roses Of Regret

Grimm Academy #14

Laura Greenwood

CONTENTS

BLURB

Rose has always lived in the shadow of her sister, but when it comes to their prophecy, it's something they both have to deal with.

When a mysterious student turns up at Rose's room, she knows it could lead to the one thing she can't let happen, especially as it will condemn her sister as well as her. But no matter how much she knows she needs to resist, she can't stop herself from falling for his charms.

Can she escape her prophecy before it's too late?

-

Roses Of Regret is part of the Grimm Academy series. It includes a sweet m/f romance.

CHAPTER 1

A loud cheer sounds from around the stadium as one of the jousters unseats the other. I don't really understand the rules of the game, but that's because it doesn't interest me very much. The only reason I'm out in the stands is the visiting students from Perault Academy. We haven't had visitors like this very often before, but the headmistress is talking about all of the academies coming together more in a chance to promote working together.

I guess it makes sense. Especially with the officers-in-training move between several of them.

So now the sports teams are competing against one another. I suspect it's only a short amount of time before we start having joint balls. I'm not sure whether I like the idea or not. It brings a lot of people onto the academy grounds and I can't help but think that'll cause a spike in prophecies starting to come true.

Including mine. Well, the prophecy I share with my twin sister.

Maybe. We can probably avoid it if we don't talk to any bears. I've always wondered about that part of our prophecy. Mostly because it doesn't make any sense. I've never seen a real bear so it seems unlikely my prophecy will have anything to do with one. The bear is probably symbolic of something. Which only adds another layer of confusion and mystery to the whole thing.

"Rose?" Zerrin prompts from beside me.

"Hmm? Sorry, I was lost in thought."

She smiles reassuringly at me. "I was just asking where Blanche had gotten to."

I frown and glance around for my twin. She's always off doing her own thing. She got all of her boldness and mine too. I don't mind too much.

"I'm sure she'll show up," I assure my friend. "You know what she's like."

Zerrin smiles and leans back in her chair, more relaxed than she used to be. Meeting Prince Andrew and stopping her prophecy from coming true have done wonders for how she feels.

I hope it does the same to me once mine is over. Despite how scary it is to think about my prophecy starting to come true, a part of me still wants it to happen, that way I can have the peace Zerrin clearly has and get on with my life.

Maybe I can even find love once it's over.

I push the thought out of my mind. It isn't worth obsessing over. These things happen when they happen.

"How long do you think the Perault students will be here?" she asks.

"I don't know. Have you heard any rumours?"

"Not really. Andrew has gone to see an old childhood friend of his while the joust is going on, so I don't think they're going to be here for too long," Zerrin says.

"Even if they go back after the joust is over, it's all people are going to be talking about for weeks."

"That's true. But this is only good for the sports teams. What about those who don't play them?" Zerrin asks.

I raise an eyebrow. When did she start worrying about that kind of thing? As far as I know, her understanding of politics is even worse than mine. And with good reason. She's at Grimm Academy on a scholarship. And even though she's courting a Prince now, he's a second son and not too involved with the way his kingdom is run. I think his father is even threatening to disinherit him over his relationship with Zerrin.

"Don't look at me like that," she says. "Aren't we supposed to be here to work on the relations between the different kingdoms?"

"Among other things."

"Was it just your prophecy that got the two of you sent here? I've never asked."

I check around us to make sure no one is paying us any attention. It's not that my prophecy has to be kept a secret, but no one ever talks about them. Mostly because the risk of the wrong person hearing it is high, even in a place like this.

But Zerrin is my closest friend, other than my sister, I can tell her anything and can be certain she won't do anything to hurt me with the in-formation. The fact she's had a prophecy of her own only adds to the certainty. She knows how the waiting feels and how scary the whole situation is.

A cheer goes up as the next person enters the list. I take a sharp breath at the heraldry being hung.

A rampant bear.

Panic grips hold of me and I ball my hands into a fist.

"Rose? Are you all right?" Zerrin reaches out and places a hand on my arm.

"I'm sorry, it's just the bear." I gesture towards the lists.

She nods. "It's part of your prophecy, right?"

I frown. "How do you know that?"

"You and Blanche were talking about it before one of the balls a little while back."

"And you've waited until now to bring it up?"

She shrugs. "It hasn't come up until now."

"It's confusing. Our prophecy is about a bear who comes to seek shelter with us because a gnome is after his treasure. I know it doesn't make much sense. That's the part that worries me the most. How am I supposed to stop it from happening if it doesn't make any sense?"

"Ah, I see. So you think the bear could be the one on the crest?" A thoughtful expression crosses Zerrin's face. "I think that makes sense."

"It's the only thing that does. Blanche thinks it'll be an actual bear..."

"Which seems unlikely."

"Very," I agree. "It's hard to imagine a bear showing up at our door and talking to us. I suppose it could be a cursed bear, but that seems unlikely. Someone would probably raise the alarm before it got to our room."

"That is true. It seems fairly easy to keep a bear away if you live in the right place."

"Mmhmm. But that doesn't stop the prophecy from hanging over my head all the time." And that's part of the problem.

She reaches out and takes my hand, giving it a squeeze. "Whatever happens, we'll sort it out. You don't have to go through this alone," she promises.

"Thank you." I know she means it. And it does reassure me more than I ever thought it would. Having a friend by my side through this will make it all so much easier.

CHAPTER 2

This ball doesn't feel any different from the dozens of others I've attended while studying at Grimm. But that's not going to last for long. After the successful inter-academy jousting match last week, the headmistress has invited the older students from Perrault Academy to join us for one of our legendary balls.

And they're going to be here at any moment.

I glance around, trying to find my sister among the crowds, but as seems to be the case increasingly often these days, Blanche is nowhere to be seen. I don't think I've ever had this much of a problem finding her before and I'm not sure what to make of it now. If I didn't know her better, I'd think she's courting someone.

Zerrin walks into the ballroom on Andrew's arm, looking every inch the future princess she is. Between the gold she's learned she can spin, and the prince on her arm, she's managed to make almost everyone forget she came to Grimm as a scholarship student. Not that I mind. She deserves every moment of this. She's worked hard to get it and I'm glad people are starting to forget her past, even if it's unfair she's been judged on it up until now anyway.

I wave at them, only realising once they start heading in my direction that without Blanche, I'm the awkward person spending time with a couple when they're not really wanted. I know my friend better than that, though. She's not going to make me feel bad. That's not her style.

"It's busy already," Zerrin says as she reaches me.

"Everyone wants to be here when the Perault students arrive," I point out.

"Ah, yes. Good point. I wonder what they'll be like."

"If I have to guess, I'd say they're exactly like us. Maybe with fewer prophecies, but I bet that's the only difference." And it might not even be true. No one really knows how prophecies work. There are plenty of people who have them but have no idea about it. Some of them manage to escape, others fall into the traps left out for them. As much as I hate knowing my life could end up destroyed by a bear and a gnome, at least I'm lucky enough to know I have a prophecy, and know the details about them. I'm even luckier still to be able to come to Grimm. The academy specialises in providing students with prophecies safe spaces in which to avoid them. And it works well if the rumours are anything to go by.

I take a sip of my drink, enjoying the sweet taste of strawberry wine. It's so much better than the varieties we get at home.

Trumpets sound, stilling everyone in the ballroom. I don't think I've ever seen one of Grimm's balls this quiet. Even the dancers have stopped. It's eerie and I'm not sure I like it. Hopefully, once the other students have made their way into the ballroom, everything will start back up again and we'll be back to normal.

Three dozen people make their way inside, all of them around my age. But then again, all of the people at the ball are. There are younger students at Grimm, but they have their own events to attend. I suspect it's so they can focus on forging the right kind of bonds between us all.

Other than avoiding prophecies, the political connections are the second biggest draw for parents sending their children here.

Once the Perault students are inside, the music strikes back up and the established couples start to gravitate to the dance floor. Those of us who change dance partner depending on the song and the ball stand to the side, a little warier of how things are going to go.

"Do you want us to stay with you?" Zerrin asks.

I shake my head. "Go, dance. I'm sure Blanche will turn up soon." Or maybe not, I truly have no idea where she is.

"If you're sure..." she trails off, her attention caught by a handsome stranger walking towards us with intent.

He bows gracefully to each of us in turn. "I'm Gavrel, pleased to make your acquaintance," he says, a slight accent tinging his words. I can't place it, but that doesn't mean anything. Almost everyone comes from a different place here.

"I'm Zerrin, this is my fiancé, Andrew. And this is Rose." She gestures to each of us in turn. It's amazing to see how much confidence she's gained.

"It's a pleasure to meet you all. I was wondering if Lady Rose would like this dance?" He holds out his hand, but I can tell it's still a question.

"I'd like that," I agree, mostly because I don't want to just keep standing here and staring. And partly because I love to dance and it'll be interesting to get a chance to do it with one of the Perault students. Which is the whole point of this evening. We're supposed to mingle and get to know one another. I'm not sure if it serves any particular purpose, but I'm going to go with it.

A boyish smile breaks out over his face as I take his hand. He seems pleased about the prospect of dancing with me, which is always nice.

He leads me onto the floor along with all the other dancers. From the hopeful hesitance on a few people's faces, it seems there are a lot of new pairings tonight.

The musicians start to play a familiar song. I dip into a curtsy without thinking about whether or not Gavrel knows the steps.

He straightens from his bow and reaches for my hands, bringing me into the correct hold for the music that's starting to play. All my worries flit away as the two of us slip into the comforting movements of the dance.

Dancing with Gavrel almost feels more natural than with any of the other dance partners I've had while at Grimm despite us not having the same dance tutors. Sometimes, I think there's something undefinable about the way two people come together that can't be created when it isn't already there. And that's what I seem to have with the stranger from Perault.

The dance ends and I find myself standing in the middle of the dance floor with a wide smile on my face. Dancing is always fun, but with Gavrel, it seems to be even more so. I'm sure it's just the novelty of having new people around. Either that, or someone spiked the wine with something stronger. It's happened before, but it's unlikely.

Most students don't see the need to when the balls are so fun to begin with.

We make our way over to the refreshments table. He picks up one of the glasses and hands it to me. Our fingers brush as I take it from him, making mine tingle.

I push the sensation aside, putting it down to nothing more than the way the wine is making me feel.

"How are you finding it here?" I ask Gavrel as we take a seat at one of the small tables set up for this purpose. I'm not sure who organises the events at Grimm, but they always put a lot of thought into all of it. I never have to look far to find anything I think I need already set up.

"I can't talk for the rest of the academy, but the company is delightful."

A blush rushes over my cheeks. "I can say the same."

"But I'll have plenty of time to discover what the rest of this place is like. I'm transferring here in a few days."

"Oh?" My interest is piqued, and not just because I get to spend more time with Gavrel if he's at Grimm.

"My father is an ambassador. He's being stationed at the palace not far from here and wants to have me closer in case things go wrong."

I frown. "What kind of thing?"

He shrugs, but I can see in his eyes that he knows the answer to that. "He's a strange man."

I don't press him further on it. We've only just met, it isn't fair of me to expect answers from deep within his soul. Maybe once we've gotten to know each other a little better, he'll open up about it.

"Perhaps once I've moved my belongings in, you'd like to give me a tour of the academy?" he suggests.

An easy smile spreads over my face. "I'm sure it can be arranged, everyone is given a student guide when they first arrive here anyway. I can see if the headmistress will let me be yours."

"Is that likely?"

"I don't know, but I don't see any reason why she'd say no. She always puts the students first and this does that."

"Then I look forward to my arrival. Thank you, Rose."

I close my eyes at the sound of my name on his lips. I'm going to have to be careful I don't end up falling for the first person to pay me attention like this. But maybe that isn't a bad thing. A small part of me is excited to find out.

CHAPTER 3

I brush down my skirts, trying to move past the nerves fluttering within me. Gavrel made it very clear that he wanted me to be the one to show him around Grimm Academy, but I'm still nervous about knocking on his door and making it official. Unsurprisingly, the headmistress had no problem with my request. I suspect she was probably secretly glad of it as it saved her from having to pick another student for the role.

I need to stop being foolish and just get on with it. Mother raised me better than to cower in front of a door.

I rap on the wood a couple of times and take a step back.

The door swings open and a smile breaks out over Gavrel's face. "I see I got the most beautiful guide at Grimm."

A small giggle escapes me, it's a foreign sound and one I'm definitely not used to making, but apparently, he's bringing it out in me.

"I wouldn't know about that, you haven't been here long," I point out.

"I saw many of them at the ball. And none of the fair ladies compare to you."

I raise an eyebrow. "I'm going to have to watch out for you charming everyone, aren't I?"

"I can behave," he promises.

"I'll believe that when I see it. Is there anything you need first? Food? Drink? Something else?"

Am I babbling? I hope not, that's not a good look on anyone.

"I could eat," he responds. "Do I need anything?" He gestures to his room.

"Not unless you have somewhere to be that isn't in the castle. Everything here is provided for us."

"Excellent." He closes the door and steps into the hall alongside me.

He offers me his arm and I place my hand on his sleeve, more than familiar with the gesture.

"How long have you been here?" he asks as we set off towards the more communal parts of the castle.

The bedrooms are all housed in their own sections, with the male and female students separate. Not that it stops anyone. There are constant visits back and forth that the staff do nothing to prevent. I'm not sure if they don't care, or if they're scared of annoying the wrong person and having their parents pull the monetary contributions to the academy as a result.

"A few years. I came with my sister. I'm sure you'll meet her at some point."

"Ah, a prophecy?"

I stiffen.

"I'm sorry, that was impolite of me to ask," he says hastily. "You don't have to tell me."

"It's fine," I assure him. "I'm not used to talking about it, but it's fine. Yes, we're here because we have a prophecy about us. A lot of the students do, but not all of them." A small part of me wants to ask if he has one, but I don't want to dwell on the subject for too long.

"I heard about that. The academy's reputation precedes it."

"A lot of very influential people send their children here to avoid them," I agree. "This is the dining hall." I gesture to the left.

A few dozen students sit around eating and chatting at leisure. It's busier at more traditional meal times, but there are almost always people in here a few hours either side.

I direct Gavrel to one of the empty tables.

"When it's the mealtime rush, we queue for food. " I wave towards the counters. "But at times like this, we need to place an order with one of the servants." Who I'm sure have already noticed us sitting down and will be making their way to us in a moment. They're always very attentive. It took a while to get used to at first.

"Good to know."

As if summoned by my words, a woman in a servant's dress comes over to us. "Good afternoon, my Lady, my Lord. What can I get for you?"

"Two meals, please. And some chilled lemon water," I answer instantly.

"Of course. I'll bring it right out." She dips into a curtsy before scurrying off to the kitchens.

"I didn't think people used titles here," Gavrel asks once she's gone.

"The students and teachers don't have to, but some choose to. The servants always use them. I assume it's too ingrained into them for them to stop. No one ever tries to change their minds."

"Interesting. I'm sure it's something I'll get used to."

"What was it like at Perault?"

The servant returns with two glasses of lemon water and sets them down in front of us.

"Thank you," I say.

"At Perault, we're supposed to use titles all the time but no one really does. I think people get complacent with it and no one really wants to use titles and honorifics with their friends all the time."

"That's true. I can imagine it must be exhausting to try and keep up with what you're supposed to call hundreds of people."

"Precisely. I'm glad I'm now in a place where I don't have to keep up with all of that."

Two bowls of stew and a basket of bread appear between us, placed there by the servants.

"This looks good," Gavrel says.

"It is. The food is always good, I'm not sure where they found the cooks, but I'm sure some monarch is sad about it somewhere."

He chuckles and tears a bread roll in half, offering one of the portions to me.

I flash him a grateful smile as I take it from him. He's right, the stew does look good. My stomach rumbles, reminding me that it's been a while since I last ate.

"There you are," Blanche says as she drops herself into one of the seats next to us. I hadn't even noticed her coming into the room. I'm not sure when she got so stealthy.

Or what she's been up to. But I'm not about to ask her about that in front of someone who is a complete stranger to her.

"Gavrel, this is my sister, Blanche. Blanche, this is Gavrel. He's just transferred from Perault." I wave my hand between the two of them as I introduce them.

"Ah, I heard rumours about someone doing that after the ball. I'm not surprised Grimm convinced you, our parties are legendary." She grabs a piece of bread and dips it into my stew. "Mmm. That's good."

"It's also mine. Get your own if you want some," I counter.

Gavrel raises an eyebrow. "Are you two always like this?" he asks.

"Pretty much," Blanche responds.

"No," I correct. "Sometimes we get along."

He chuckles. "My cousins are the same way. I'm used to it."

"Are they at one of the academies?" Blanche asks, completely ignoring my suggestion of getting food for herself as she digs into mine.

"Not yet. But they both want to be," he answers. "And..."

"You were looking for me for something?" I prompt Blanche, hoping she'll leave me to have more of a private conversation with Gavrel.

"Oh, yes. Mother sent some money for dresses, I wanted to know when you were free to go into town to see the seamstress."

"Tomorrow works. I have classes in the morning, but after lunch I'm free."

"I'll meet you after then and we'll go down."

"Sounds good." And it does. It'll be nice to spend some time just the two of us, maybe she'll even tell me what she's been up to in the past few weeks that's kept her so busy.

"See you," she says as she gets to her feet and walks out of the hall, leaving me and Gavrel alone again.

"So, that's my sister," I mutter with a vague wave after her. "You'll get used to her."

"I'm sure I will."

"Once we've finished eating, I can take you on a proper tour of the castle if you want?"

He nods. "I'd like that."

"Good, then it's settled." I don't even try to suppress the joy within me that I'll get to spend more time without anyone else around so I can get to know him better. I've never felt this way about anyone else before. I hope it won't lead me into trouble.

CHAPTER 4

T he summer months are always full of events and activities, especially for the sports teams. I've never cared much about them before, other than the occasional fun walk or horse ride, but when Gavrel asked me to come to one of the jousts to give him my favour, I instantly said yes.

Perhaps I shouldn't have. But it feels right to say yes to him, even if I barely know him.

I head towards the tent where the jousting team prepares. Though calling it that isn't quite right.

The structure is a permanent one, and probably built with some kind of magic in order to help it survive against the elements.

I push thoughts of how the tent must be constructed out of my mind. It isn't like that's the most important thing for me to consider at the moment.

The fabric at the entrance flutters open. I step back to give whoever is exiting space to move.

My eyes widen as I come face to face with the last person I expected.

"Blanche?"

"Oh, Rose, there you are. What are you doing here?"

"Gavrel asked for my favours. What about you?" As far as I know, she isn't courting anyone. Could I be wrong?

An uncharacteristic blush crosses her face.

Hmm. Maybe I am wrong. Blanche isn't the kind of person who cares what others think. If she's feeling caught out about what she's doing, there must be a good reason for it.

"I'm on an errand," she mutters.

I narrow my eyes but I don't say anything. If she isn't ready to talk about what she's doing, it's fine. I'm sure she'll reveal the truth when she's ready to.

"Are you going to be watching from the stands?" I ask.

"Of course." Relief flashes over her face as she realises I'm not going to press her any further on the subject.

"I'll just talk to Gavrel and then I'll come to find you." I smile reassuringly at her.

"All right."

I frown as I watch her walk away. She's not acting like herself at the moment and it's starting to worry me. What if something's happened to start our prophecy and she's worrying about it alone?

No. That can't be the case. The prophecy is something we share, she wouldn't keep something so important from me.

I try not to dwell on it as I push through the tent flap.

The various members of the jousting team are getting ready for their turn on the lists. It's just a friendly match within the team itself, but with the good weather, events like this can draw quite a crowd of students who want to sit in the sun while being entertained.

I scan the faces to try and find Gavrel. I've never been inside the tent before and have no idea which spot belongs to which team member.

"Rose!" he calls, waving at me from across the room.

I hurry over, anxious to see him. I know it hasn't been long since we met, but I enjoy his company and long for the moments we can share together.

"Are you almost ready?" I ask, taking in the well-fitted armour he's wearing. It looks as if he's got everything he needs on, but I don't know enough about it to be completely sure.

"Nearly. I just need to do up some of these ties." He gestures with his arm revealing dangling tassels.

"Would you like me to do it?" The question escapes before I can think through how close that'll bring me to him.

"If you don't mind."

He stands still while I reach around for the ties. The move brings us closer together than I'd anticipated. It's not exactly proper for a young lady of my station to do this, but no one is here to stop me. I'm not sure whether it's the academy's aim to make it happen, or if it's a byproduct of giving us all a little bit more independence. Whatever the reason, I'm going to take advantage of it.

Neither of us says anything as I close the ties, securing his armour more tightly. I'm sure he'll have to double-check it once I've finished. I certainly hope he does. I don't want to be responsible for part of his armour falling off mid-joust.

I don't move away from him when I'm done, wishing to savour the moment. "I think I'm done." My voice comes out hoarser than I expect it to.

I clear my throat and take a step back.

"Thank you," he whispers.

A bell tolls, making me jump. "What was that for?" I ask, looking around the assembled jousters to see what they're doing. A few of them seem to be moving towards the entrance.

"It's the signal for the first joust," he says. "Nothing to worry about. I still have a few minutes."

"Then we should finish getting you ready."

I reach for the sleeve of my gown where a satin ribbon is threaded through the fabric. I tug on it until it pulls away from the loops holding it in place. The sleeve looks bare without it, but I know this is what it's designed for. Some ladies still prefer to carry favours in their pockets rather than pull apart their dresses, but I don't have anything I can use that way. I've never been asked for one before.

"Here."

Gavrel holds out his arm, his gaze meeting mine as I slip the ribbon around it and tie it tightly. He reaches out and tucks it into the armour so it isn't in the way.

"Thank you."

"You asked for it," I point out.

"I know. But you didn't have to give it to me."

I rest my hand on his breastplate. "I wanted to."

A small smile stretches over his face as he looks down at me.

The bell sounds again, but it doesn't make me jump this time.

"Do you need to go?"

"I do. But we can go for something to eat after, if you'd like?"

"Only so long as you win," I tease.

"When I have a favour from you, there's no way I won't."

A small laugh escapes me. "I may not be the good luck charm you think I am."

"I guess we'll see in about five minutes."

"Good luck." On a whim, I go up onto my toes and press a soft kiss against his cheek.

His smile widens into a grin. "I'll see you after."

I nod eagerly.

He heads away from me and towards the line of shields propped up on a wooden trolley. Gavrel leans down to pick one up and my blood runs cold.

A rampant bear frolics across his shield.

I've done the unthinkable and invited a bear into my life and triggered the prophecy that could be my undoing. And my sister's.

CHAPTER 5

I flop down onto the bench beside Zerrin and try not to make an undignified sound.

She raises an eyebrow. "That bad?" She gestures for one of the servants to bring us an extra teacup and pushes the plate of biscuits in my direction.

"I don't even know," I admit. "Maybe if I could find my sister, I'd be able to talk it through and decide."

Zerrin purses her lips as if trying to decide what to say. "You can talk to me, if you want," she offers.

"I know you might not want to. But the offer is there if you want it to be. I may not know you quite like Blanche does, but I'd like to think I've done a good job at getting to know you."

"You have," I start. "It's just..."

"This is about your prophecy. I already figured that much."

The servant arrives and places the second cup on the table silently. I'm not sure if she can tell what kind of conversation we're having, or if she acts that way around everyone, but I'm grateful. It's hard enough to talk about such a potentially horrible thing as it is.

"How?"

"The look on your face. And the fact you started talking about it the other day," she points out. "Besides, it wouldn't be Gavrel, the two of you are positively sickening together."

I snort. "Because you're any better."

"Exactly. I know how you're feeling right now, I've been there. Though I have to admit, I'm surprised at how easily you're admitting there's something between the two of you."

"It would be pointless of me to deny it." Especially to Zerrin. She's very observant when it comes to just about everything. Though she doesn't have any more ideas about what Blanche is up to than I do.

"All right, so spill. What's the problem?" She picks up the pot and begins pouring tea into my cup. She doesn't even have to ask how I like it. She already knows.

A wave of affection towards my friend travels through me.

"Do you remember the bear shield at the jousting match?" I ask.

"Mmhmm. You didn't like it because of what you thought it might mean." She sets the pot down and pours in a dash of milk before holding out the cup and saucer to me.

I flash her a grateful smile, albeit a fleeting one. "It's Gavrel's."

Understanding crosses her face. "Ah."

"Yes."

"I can see how that could be a bit of a problem."

I take a sip of my tea, noticing it's the perfect temperature for drinking already. That's definitely one of the advantages of sitting down with someone who already had a pot brewed.

"And it means Gavrel is part of your prophecy."

I sigh. "Yes. That's the part I'm worried about. My prophecy never says anything about romance..." I set my cup down gently.

"Your prophecy also talks about a bear wanting you to let him into your bedroom," she points out. "I don't think we can take anything in your prophecy at face value."

I slump back in my seat. "Why do you have to be so right?"

"It's an annoying habit I've picked up," she quips.

A soft snort escapes me. "Do you know how hard it is to have a prophecy written in riddles?"

She arches an eyebrow. "Surprisingly, I do."

I sigh. "I'm sorry. I'm being very woe is me."

"It's fine. I remember realising my prophecy had started. I've never felt fear like that before." A shiver runs down her spine. "But there's still time. We're going to get you through this. Most people don't get rid of their prophecies until they're about to start."

"I know you're right." But it doesn't make me want to deal with it any more than before. It doesn't help that I'm starting to worry about Blanche and how she's going to cope with this if she isn't around to even know. As much as I'd love it if the prophecy wouldn't come true just because she isn't aware of what's happening, I don't think that's how it works.

"Remind me what your prophecy says about the bear?" Zerrin says.

"Why?"

"A hunch. Humour me?"

"A bear wants to come into our room or house. He doesn't ask much of us, just for some shelter and company."

"Right, so the bear doesn't do anything bad in your prophecy?" she prompts.

I scrunch up my face as I consider what she's saying. "I've never thought about it like that."

"So, what's the problem with the bear?" She reaches out for a biscuit and takes a big bite, crunching on it as she waits for me to answer.

"I guess there isn't one," I admit. "But I've always thought about the prophecy as one thing, not as separate parts."

"Then you need to change that." Zerrin brushes a smattering of crumbs off her dress. "Think about it in parts. To me, it sounds like the bear is just the thing that signals your prophecy is nearing."

"Maybe."

"More than maybe. It's the dwarf that causes the problem, right?"

"Yes," I draw the word out more than I have to, mostly because I'm only just starting to process what she's saying. "Which means the bear is fine."

"Mmhmm. That's great news for you."

Confusion rushes through me. "I'm not sure I follow you anymore."

"It means you can carry on doing whatever it is you and Gavrel are doing to avoid admitting you want to court each other. You'll have to keep an eye out for any evidence of the dwarf who plans to...wait, what does he plan to do?"

"Steal the bear's treasure."

"Interesting. Maybe you're the treasure," Zerrin muses.

"I hardly doubt that. I barely have a title. Most people will pass over me when it comes to a poten-tial marriage alliance because of it."

"Oh, Rose." Her exasperation is plain in her voice. "The rest of your prophecy isn't literal, maybe the treasure isn't either? It could just be that the dwarf wants to steal something important from Gavrel. That could be you, not treasure of the glittering kind."

"I hardly think I'm worth more than jewels."

Zerrin smiles sadly. "Don't sell yourself short. I imagine Gavrel sees you as far more valuable. I know I do, and I can spin straw into gold."

"Maybe that just makes treasure worthless," I mutter.

She lets out a light-hearted laugh. "Maybe it does. But in all honesty, I'd give up the ability and everything it's brought me so long as I got to keep our friendship and my relationship with Andrew. People are worth far more than all the riches in the world."

Something about the way she says it makes me reach out and take her hand in mine to give it a squeeze.

"You don't have to give up anything to keep me as your friend," I promise.

"I'm glad. But you can't give up whatever it is you have with Gavrel because of your prophecy. If you do, then it's truly won."

"You're far too wise these days."

"Only when it comes to this."

"Thank you, Zerrin."

"Any time," she promises. "I'm serious. I'm always here if you need to talk. And I promise I won't always say you're wrong."

I snort. "It's fine if you do. I clearly needed to hear it."

"Yes. You did."

"All right, that's enough now."

"You've got it. Why don't you go find Gavrel before class starts again? You have an hour, that should be enough time to talk to him while still being able to get away before things get too intense," she says.

"Thank you." I rise to my feet, not even finishing my tea.

She's right. I do need to go find Gavrel. I've only been avoiding him since this morning and I already feel awful. It isn't fair to him to keep him in the dark about what's going on, especially when it's about something as important as a prophecy.

Besides, it isn't his fault he's part of mine. Maybe if I talk to him about it, he may have some helpful ideas about who or what the dwarf in my prophecy may be. Especially as I very much doubt it's a real dwarf. That would be too easy. And if there's one thing I've learned about prophecies, it's that there isn't an easy way out of them.

CHAPTER 6

"Hello," I say as I approach Gavrel where he's seated in the food hall.

"Ah, I see you've stopped avoiding me." His lips lift into a smile, but there's a sadness in his expression that I can't ignore. Especially as I'm the one who caused it. That's not fair to Gavrel when he didn't do anything wrong.

"I'm sorry," I say softly. "Do you mind if I sit down?"

"Are you going to explain why you've been avoiding me?"

"Yes."

"Then of course you can."

I manage a weak smile and slide onto the bench opposite him, rearranging my skirts so they don't catch on anything.

"You don't have any food."

"I don't think I'll be able to enjoy it until we've talked," I admit. "I really am sorry."

"It's fine, Rose. But it was a little bit unexpected."

I sigh. "I know."

"Did I do something wrong?"

"No."

"Then what happened?"

"It was your shield." My voice comes out as barely more than a whisper. Other than my family and Zerrin, I've never talked to anyone about my prophecy. And I certainly never thought I'd be talking to one of the people involved in it.

He frowns, pushing his plate away. "My shield?"

"Your crest is a bear, right?"

"Yes."

I take a deep breath. This would be so much easier if prophecies weren't treated as such mysterious things. If we learned how to talk about them, we wouldn't have to worry about how to share with people.

"My prophecy is about a bear," I say. There's no way to put this in a better way, I just have to get it all out there.

"Ah." Understanding crosses his face. "And you think I'm going to do something bad to you?"

"No," I blurt out quickly. "I don't think anything of the sort."

"All right..."

"The bear in my prophecy is friendly, as far as any of us know. He's supposed to be the indication that it's starting." I fiddle with the beading on my dress, trying to distract myself from the pounding in my head. I never expected to have this conversation.

Maybe I should have talked to Blanche about this first, but she seems to have disappeared again. I'm not sure what's going on with my sister, but I'm sure she'll tell me eventually.

"The bear is supposed to need shelter and protection from a dwarf. I have no idea what that means."

He frowns.

So it appears he doesn't understand the meaning either. I'm not sure whether that's reassuring or not.

"It's the dwarf that causes problems."

"It sounds very cryptic."

"Incredibly so. There's no indication that the bear is even a person. It wasn't until I saw your shield that I started to put two and two together."

"So you think the dwarf might be to do with a shield too?" he asks.

I shrug. "I honestly have no idea." I glance down at the table, feeling somewhat ashamed of how little I actually know about my own prophecy. It could destroy my entire life and I have no idea what half of it even means. "Do you know anyone with a dwarf on their heraldry?"

He shakes his head. "I don't know anyone who it could relate to. I'm sorry."

I let out a loud sigh. "It's fine. I didn't expect you to."

"I can't imagine how scary this is for you," he says, reaching out and taking my hand in his.

I manage a weak smile. "I feel better having talked about it with people I trust."

"I hope you're including me in that number."

"Of course. My friend Zerrin too. You've doubled the number of people who know about it."

He chuckles. "Your twin..." he trails off, the question hanging in the air between us.

"It's a shared prophecy. It's about both of us."

"I heard they're rare."

"As far as I'm aware, but no one talks about these things. I'm sure you know that."

"I do. You're the first person who has ever told me about their prophecy."

"You're only the second person who I've ever told myself, so I can see how that's true."

He gives my hand a squeeze. "I'll do anything I possibly can to help you with this," he promises. "I know I haven't been very helpful yet, but I will be."

"Thank you. I really appreciate it. I'm sure Blanche will too."

The earnestness in his eyes is impossible to ignore. He means every word, and I'm glad about that. If I'm going to survive this, then I'm going to need all of the help I can get. And like Zerrin pointed out, even in my prophecy, the bear doesn't do anything to hurt me. Gavrel is just proving that's true.

CHAPTER 7

Whispers pass around the corridors faster than anything else at Grimm Academy, particularly when there's something exciting happening.

Nobody seems to be paying me much attention as I enter the dining room with Gavrel, which means everyone is still in the dark about my prophecy, which is a small mercy. I don't want to have to deal with the pitying looks and the relieved sighs that come with anyone living through their prophecy. I've seen it happen too many times with other students to know it won't be the case.

My gaze lands on my sister and my heart lifts at the sight. I feel like it's ages since I last saw her despite living in the next room.

"Come on, let's go join Blanche," I say, tugging Gavrel towards the table.

"Hi," Blanche says as I sit down opposite her.

"What's going on?" I ask, gesturing to the hall around us.

Gavrel sits down next to me and gestures to the closest serving girl so we can order some food and tea.

Blanche shrugs. "There's a new student coming."

"That happens all the time, it never gets this much attention." Students come and go fairly regularly, both to fulfil their duties to their kingdoms, and starting and ending their studies. With all the kingdoms having different traditions and celebrations, the academy finds it easier to let everyone come and go as they please and keep the castle open all year round for the people who aren't needed elsewhere. I'm sure there are quieter months, but I haven't noticed anything. They probably happen around the same time as Blanche and I are called home to take part in the Yuletide celebrations.

"It's a transfer," she says.

My eyes widen. "Another one?" I glance at Gavrel.

"Don't look at me, I don't know anything about it."

"Oh." I try not to be too disappointed by that.

"They're transferring in from Perault," Blanche says. "You might know them."

"I might, but no one was talking about making the transfer," Gavrel says.

"That's a shame, it would have been good to be the first person who knows something," Blanche says wistfully.

I shake my head in bemusement. It's not like it would do us any good to know who is transferring.

I glance at Gavrel again.

Or maybe it will. For all I know, the person coming to Grimm Academy is the dwarf from our prophecy. I'm not sure how that would work, but I never expected to find the bear in a person either.

"We'll find out soon enough," I assure my sister. "The moment they step foot in the castle, we'll know their name and their family tree. You know what it's like." Half the time, the new arrivals are the ones talking about who they're related to and how powerful they are.

A serving girl sets down a bowl of stew in front of me, and another in front of Gavrel. The savoury meat smell wafts up to my nose, making my stomach rumble. I don't think I realised how hungry I am.

"It's good," Blanche promises, her own empty bowl testament to that.

Gavrel is already digging into the bowl. He's had jousting practice this morning, so is probably hungrier than me.

A lot of shouting comes from the direction of the door. At first, it's easy to ignore, but the chatter increases by the second.

I twist around to see what's going on to find a gaggle of girls around the entrance.

"What..." I trail off as the crowd parts to reveal one of the most handsome guys our age I've ever seen. "Who is that?" I whisper.

He's tall with dark hair and a killer smile which lights up the room even from this distance.

"Ah, Hugo," Gavrel mutters, clearly a little annoyed by the new arrival.

"He's the transfer student?" I ask.

"Yes. And all the girls at Perault fawned over him too. I guess I'll have to put up with it here too."

Blanche glances up and makes a non-committal noise. "He's nothing special."

A soft snort escapes from Gavrel. "Can you tell everyone else that?"

"I don't think they're going to believe me."

"Even Rose?" Blanche smirks.

"I'm not blindsided by him," I snap. "He's just a handsome guy."

Gavrel's shoulders slump and I realise what I've done.

I reach out and put a gentle hand on his arm. "But he's nothing compared to you in my eyes," I say softly.

Blanche laughs, but covers her mouth with her hand. "Sorry. You're just sickening."

I roll my eyes and ignore her. Sometimes, I think it would be easier not to be a twin, but there's nothing I can do to change that. Nor do I really want to. I love Blanche and can't imagine my life without her.

"Who is he?" I ask Gavrel, hoping he'll provide more information. Not so I can do anything about it, but because it will be good to know when other people talk.

"His name's Hugo Klein. He's the son of a marquis who doesn't have much of a political standing, but is incredibly wealthy which makes up some of the difference."

"That explains why everyone is so interested in him," Blanche mutters.

"Do you know why he's transferred?" I take another bite of my stew. It's delicious as normal.

"I imagine it'll be something to do with his marriage prospects. I heard his parents are keen on him marrying up and there weren't as many eligible princesses at Perault as there are here," Gavrel responds.

"So we should expect a proposal within a week," Blanche suggests.

"Maybe not, his family may be disappointed that Princess Briar is spoken for," I counter. I'm sure a crown princess would count as a good catch for most people.

Gavrel chuckles. "I'm not sure. He's about as arrogant as he looks."

"Insufferable then."

I shoot a warning look at my sister. We shouldn't be overheard talking badly about anyone. Our family isn't well known or well connected enough for us to be able to recover from that.

"I wouldn't worry about it. He'll find something to distract him in a day or so," Gavrel says.

I hope he's right. As interesting as it is to have a new person around, I like the way my life is going at the moment. Other than the prophecy, that is.

Hopefully, the new student won't make things worse as far as that's concerned.

CHAPTER 8

The breeze ruffles through my hair and tugs at the spare fabric of my dress as I walk arm in arm with Gavrel through the grounds of the academy.

"Are you sure you don't want to do anything else?" he asks.

I shake my head. "I love seeing the flowers," I admit. "It's peaceful."

"Very well."

"Unless you want to do something else? Would you rather we were inside playing chess?"

He chuckles. "I only want to be where I can spend more time with you. Why don't we spend our time outside while the good weather is with us, and when it turns colder we'll go inside for a game of chess."

"That sounds lovely," I agree.

"Then it's settled. A beautiful walk with an equally beautiful woman."

A blush rises to my cheeks at his words. I'm not sure which part of his statement it is that has me blushing, but there's something wonderful about the way he makes me feel. No one has ever treated me like I'm this precious before.

A small part of me wants to ask him what we're doing. We've yet to put a name to this, but we should. I'm spending more time with him than I am with either Blanche or Zerrin. That has to mean something.

But I'm too scared to ask and start the conversation. Maybe when there's a better opening than now.

"How are you finding Grimm?" I ask. "Is everyone treating you well?"

He nods. "Everyone's forgotten I haven't been here long, I think Hugo's arrival made them all forget."

"It's not a bad thing,"I say softly. "I've seen how everyone can get when they think someone is new."

"Oh, I'm not complaining. If I can blend in and not be the subject of gossip, then that's fine by me."

"That was always going to be the case," I reassure him. "Even without Hugo. Someone's prophecy would have started happening." Maybe even my own. It's best not to think about that too much.

A figure approaches from a distance, but I can't work out who it is. I don't think it matters. Students are always in one area of the castle or another, especially those around my age who have a bit more free time. The younger students study in a different part of the grounds and we rarely see them.

"It's nicer here than at Perault," he admits. "People are much more focused on titles there. They'll treat everyone who is even one step below them with contempt. I imagine that's why Hugo transferred. His family might have a lot of money and the power that comes with it, but their title puts him very far down the pecking order."

"It must be frustrating."

"Very."

"I dread to think how low down Blanche and I would be at Perault. Our family title isn't a particularly high up one."

"But you have your beauty and charm to make up for it," Gavrel counters. "That can get you further up."

"It sounds exhausting. At least most people here actually take the time to get to know one another."

"I don't disagree," he says. "There's a lot of trying to remember who to use what honorific for. I swear I learned more about that than any of my lessons. I'm glad Father decided to move me here so I was closer to him, it means I can actually learn the things I need to get ahead once I leave."

"I'm glad he transferred you too," I admit softly. "It allows me to have the pleasure of your company.

Gavrel chuckles. "I must admit that is the best part."

The figure is closer now. He waves at us and hurries closer still. It takes me a moment to recognise the tall build.

Hugo.

Great. Everyone is talking about him constantly, I'd hoped to be able to escape him for most of the walk.

"Gavrel, I didn't realise this was where you'd transferred to," he says by way of greeting.

My walking partner gives him a tight smile, clearly less than impressed to have our walk interrupted.

I squeeze my hand tighter on his arm in a hope that it reassures him I feel the same.

"Yes, I started just before you," Gavrel says stiffly. "How are you finding Grimm?"

"Excellent, everyone is welcoming. And they aren't judging me for not gaining my proper title yet."

Gavrel's scowl deepens.

I step closer. I don't know what this is about, but he clearly needs some support.

"Who is your friend, I don't think I've had the pleasure of meeting her?" Hugo says, turning to me with a slight leer in his eyes. But there's something more than that behind it. Almost as if he's afraid of me. But I have no idea why that may be.

"This is Lady Rose," Gavrel says. "Rose, this is Master Hugo Klein."

I raise an eyebrow. I didn't expect him to use our titles. Or in Hugo's case, his lack of one. Maybe it's something to do with the way he opened the conversation.

"It's good to meet you." I incline my head but I don't extend my hand.

"A pleasure, Rose."

Gavrel's displeasure becomes even more pronounced. I need to get us out of this situation.

"I have a class to get to. Would you mind escorting me, Gavrel?" I ask.

He nods curtly. "Excuse us."

"Of course, I don't want to keep a beautiful lady from her studies," Hugo says. Charm exudes from every part of him, something I'm sure many people enjoy. But I don't. Something is very off about it. I don't like it at all.

I dip my head again as I lead Gavrel past the other student. I'm not sure what about him is affecting Gavrel as much as it is, but I'm sure he'll tell me once we're out of earshot.

"What class do you have?" Gavrel asks. "I thought you had the rest of the afternoon free."

"I do. But it seemed as if you wanted to get away from Hugo, so I thought I'd help."

A wide grin spreads over his face. "Thank you."

I check over my shoulder to make sure we're out of Hugo's earshot. "You're welcome. But are you all right?"

"I will be," he promises.

"That doesn't do anything to reassure me," I point out.

Gavrel sighs. "Hugo's family are in line to inherit my family title after me."

"What? Why?"

"An ill advised wager on the part of my grandfather."

"Ah, I see. And Hugo wants what isn't his."

"Precisely. There are terms attached about when that title is forfeit and it's coming close. I honestly forgot about it until just now."

I nod, my thoughts churning. "Could that be the something precious from my prophecy?" I whisper.

Horror flits over Gavrel's face as the possibility sinks in. "I'm so sorry, I never even thought..."

I place my spare hand on his arm in what I hope is a comforting gesture. "It's my problem to think about."

"But you asked me and I said I had no idea."

"Gavrel, it's fine," I say softly. "There's been a lot going on. I don't blame you for not thinking of it. You've told me now, that's what matters. So you think he's the representation of the dwarf in my prophecy?"

"There's a chance of it," he agrees. "His family name means little. It isn't a literal translation, but who knows."

"Well, your bear was metaphorical. I've been assuming the dwarf is too." I glance over my shoulder, but Hugo is already out of sight.

"We'll figure it out," Gavrel promises. "Whatever happens."

I smile weakly. "I know." But I need to talk to my sister. She's been very out of the loop with our prophecy and everything that's been going on and it's time to change that.

CHAPTER 9

I hurry out of my room and towards the wooden door next to mine. I don't bother knocking. It's early and while I know Blanche will already be up, I don't have to worry about disturbing her. She never does anything before breakfast. She says it's because she likes to wake up in a leisurely fashion, but I'm not so sure.

Right now, I'm not going to question it too much as it plays to my advantage.

I only discover how wrong my assumption is once the door swings open.

Blanche springs back from the person sitting on her bed as if I've caught her doing something she shouldn't be. Which I suppose she is if I go by the rules of the academy. Not so much if I think about her happiness first and foremost. No one cares about the academy rules of not having boys in our rooms, not even the academy staff.

Except the person next to Blanche isn't one of the boys. It's Joan.

Understanding dawns on me. That's why Blanche was in the jousting tent the day I saw Gavrel's crest. She was meeting one of the jousters, but it wasn't one of the boys, it was the only female member of the team.

Clearly this is something we're going to need to talk about at some point. I want to hear everything about how they realised they wanted to court one another. Assuming that's what they're doing.

But there's no other explanation for moving away from one another so fast.

"I'm sorry for interrupting," I say once I realise I'm standing in the entrance to my sister's room and staring. "I can come back later."

I turn to leave. As much as I want to talk to Blanche, I wouldn't want her hanging around if I was in a similar situation.

"No, please stay," Blanche responds. "Joan was just leaving for early morning practice. I don't know how she manages to do it every morning."

The other girl laughs uncomfortably. "If I don't, they won't let me stay on the team. I have to work twice as hard to get even a little bit of the recognition."

Blanche sighs. "That's terribly unfair. You're just as good as them."

"I know. But if I want to challenge the norm, then I have to play by their rules." Joan gets to her feet and hesitates as if she wants to kiss Blanche goodbye. "I'll see you after lunch?" she says instead.

"I'll be waiting," Blanche promises.

"It's good to see you, Rose," she says to me as she passes and leaves the room.

"So, I'm guessing that's why you've been hard to find recently." I make my way over to Blanche's bed and take a seat next to her.

A blush rises to her cheeks, which is a new one. I don't think I've ever seen her respond to a question like that before.

"I suppose I have been a little preoccupied," she admits.

"Do you want to talk about it?"

"There's not much to say."

"Because you don't think I'll be interested, or you don't want to tell me?" I don't know which answer will hurt more, but this is about her.

She frowns. "When you put it like that, I don't know."

I reach out and take my sister's hand in mine, giving it a reassuring squeeze. "That's all right. We don't have to talk about it at all if you don't want to. But I'm here if you change your mind."

She flashes me a weak smile, seemingly a little unconvinced. "Thanks." She shifts on the bed so she's facing me. "You came bursting in here, what did you want to tell me?"

"Maybe I just wanted to say hello."

She raises an eyebrow. "I'd like to think I know you better than that. You had your I-need-to-talk-to-you face on."

I let out a soft sigh. She isn't wrong.

"It's about our prophecy."

"Please tell me you're not panicking about it again? We'll be fine. Whenever it comes along, we'll deal with it and nothing bad will happen," she reassures me in a surprisingly calm tone for her. Normally she's more exasperated by my concerns. Perhaps it's the guilt over not being around much recently.

"It's not unnecessary panic. Or any panic, really," I say quickly before she can start trying to tell me not to worry about it more. "But it's very real."

"I know," she promises. "The prophecies are real and can affect our future..."

"It's more than that," I put in quickly. "Ours is here."

"At Grimm? I kind of guessed that. I'm not sure how they do it, but a lot of prophecies seem to start once students start here. If they didn't manage to divert so many prophecies too, I'd think the academy was trying to make them happen."

"I mean time wise. Our prophecy is happening now."

Blanche's eyes widen. "How do you know?"

"Gavrel's the bear. Well, not a real one."

"I did think he was a little hairless for a bear," she quips as if it isn't a situation that could end very badly for us.

"His crest is a bear."

"Right. And you're still courting him?"

"We're not courting," I mutter.

"You're acting like you are."

I try not to let my disappointment about that show on my face. "We haven't talked about it yet."

"You should. But carry on. He's the bear. That's not terrible. The bear is supposed to be nice."

"Gavrel is nice."

"I agree," Blanche says. "But that's not the entire part of our prophecy."

"The new student?"

"Hugo?"

"Yes, Hugo Klein. We think he's the metaphorical dwarf," I say.

"You've talked to Gavrel about this, haven't you?" she asks, not sounding too surprised.

"Yes. I'm sorry, I just find it easy to open up to him."

"It's fine. I feel the same around Joan."

Oh, good. She's starting to open up to me about what's going on there, even if it's only by little comments.

"Hugo is after Gavrel's family title."

"The treasure," Blanche mutters.

"We think so. But maybe we're wrong."

"I don't think so," she says. "That feels right."

"But it doesn't help with what we need to do to stop our prophecy from coming true," I point out.

"No, maybe not. But a lot of the students who have prophecies say the way out came to them."

I bite my bottom lip. Do I just want to take a chance and hope for the best when it comes to something as important as this? That doesn't sound great, especially when it could risk Gavrel losing out too. It isn't even his prophecy, he shouldn't be badly affected by it, that wasn't fair.

Blanche squeezes my hand. "We'll work it out, Rose," she promises. "You don't have anything to worry about."

"People keep saying that."

"Probably because we're smart," she points out. "But you have to remember that you don't have to go through this alone."

"I know you're with me through this."

"I didn't even mean me," she responds. "We have Gavrel and Joan to help us. And you know as well as I do that Zerrin would be by our side in a second if she thought there was something she could do to help. We'll get through this and stop the worst from happening. Just watch and see."

Despite us not being any further forward in working out precisely what was going on with our prophecy, her words are reassuring. I feel like between us, we can beat this, even if I'm not sure exactly how.

CHAPTER 10

I search the ballroom for Gavrel, unsure where he's gotten to. He had jousting practice until late and said he'll join us at the ball when he's done.

I hope he won't be long, especially as Blanche has already disappeared with Joan. Not that I mind. Now I know what she's doing and who she's with, her absences make a lot more sense. And if that's what she needs to explore their courtship, then that's what she should do.

I hope we get more opportunities for the two of us to talk about it. I don't think we've ever both been courting someone at the same time before.

"Lady Rose, it's a pleasure to see you again," a somewhat familiar voice says.

I spin around, my ball gown flaring pleasantly as I do. I always used to imagine this move when I was a little girl. Surprisingly, it lives up to the daydreaming.

"Lord Klein, it's good to see you again." Or not. But it's best not to voice opinions like that out loud. The academy has events like this so that the students can form connections, not so we can insult one another.

One wrong word can still lead to a war, even if no one wants to voice that opinion out loud.

"I'm not a Lord yet," he says.

"I was being polite." I force a pleasant smile on my face, but the only thing I can think about is that the person in front of me is hoping to steal Gavrel's title from him. I don't want that to happen. And not just because I like Gavrel, it's also a generally horrible move.

"If you were being extra polite, you'd agree to a dance." There's a spark in his eyes I'm not so keen on, but I can't really say anything about it.

"I'm waiting for someone, maybe later?" I suggest.

"For Gavrel? He was still on the lists last time I saw."

Disappoint floods through me, and from the gleeful expression on Hugo's face, I don't do very well at hiding it.

"I take it you're free for a dance now?"

"I'm sorry, I'm not," I say firmly.

"Because you're courting someone?"

My gaze flits to the ballroom entrance, hoping to see Gavrel entering.

Sadly, he hasn't appeared to come and save me from this situation. I push the thought aside. I'm not in need of saving by anyone. I can do it myself.

"Of sorts," I respond.

I've been thinking about what Gavrel and I are doing as courting, but now I'm faced with the question, I realise we haven't actually talked about it. And I don't want to confirm something that may not be true. Sure, he's given me all of the signals, but that doesn't mean I get to tell other people what we are without at least trying to talk to him about it first.

"My friend needs me," I say, having spotted Zerrin from across the dancefloor. She doesn't actually need me to do anything, but I know she won't turn me away when I need her.

"Ah, so no dance."

"I'm afraid not this time." I try to smile, but I'm sure it doesn't reach my eyes.

Hugo isn't doing anything bad, but something about the interaction is making me uncomfortable, and I want to avoid making that worse if I can.

"I'll find you later to claim the promised dance," he responds with a sharp nod of his head.

I grimace. Hopefully, he doesn't hold me to that or I'm going to have to point out I never made any kind of promise about it. If I'm lucky, Gavrel will turn up soon and I'll be able to keep busy with him.

"I really need to go," I say without confirming or denying his statement. I need to get out of this situation quickly, and before it ends up getting worse.

I slip away and head towards where Zerrin is chatting to one of our other classmates.

She sees me coming, her face lighting up. She makes her excuses and turns to face me, a frown pulling at her features as soon as we're level.

"What's wrong?" she asks.

"I'll tell you in a minute. Where's Andrew?" I respond, searching around for her prince.

"He's back in his kingdom for the week on business. I thought you knew?"

I shake my head. "Or maybe I did and I forgot."

"Rose, what's wrong?" she asks.

I sigh. "The normal stuff."

"Prophecy or Blanche?"

"Blanche is fine. She's been courting someone but keeping it quiet."

Zerrin raises an eyebrow. "I feel like there's a story there."

"Me too, but she hasn't told me what it is yet. I'm hoping she will." Which is true. But I won't reveal any part of my sister's secret without knowing she's comfortable having it shared. Our prophecy is one thing. Her potential relationship with Joan is another.

My friend nods. "I'm sure she will. So that means it's about your prophecy?"

"Kind of. How did you know you and Andrew were courting?"

Zerrin frowns and cocks her head to the side. "Just a feeling, at first. And then after a bit we talked about it, but by the time the conversation came around it was already obvious where we were heading."

I nod, relieved to hear her say that. I realise that each relationship between two people is different, but it's still good to hear. Zerrin and Andrew have been happy for a good while now, I trust that she knows what she's talking about.

I glance over my shoulder to where Hugo had been standing when I'd left him. He's gone now, presumably to go bother someone else.

To save any situations like that again, I need to talk to Gavrel about this soon. Hopefully, I haven't read the situation wrong and he feels the same about me as I do about him.

CHAPTER 11

"How are things with Joan?" I ask Blanche as we turn the corner, the gravel path crunching beneath our boots as we do a lap around the forest on the grounds of Grimm Academy. It's a nice walk this time of year, especially if you want to have private conversations.

Blanche sighs dreamily, which isn't a sound I think I've ever heard her make before. She must be really smitten. "It's wonderful," she admits.

"I'm glad. You deserve someone."

"I know."

I laugh ever so softly at her self-assuredness, but secretly admire it. She isn't wrong. She does deserve someone who cares about her like Joan clearly does.

"When did..."

My question is cut off by a blood-curdling scream from the forest.

I exchange a worried glance with my sister before setting off into the trees to find the source of it. Whoever is there must be in a lot of pain. While I wouldn't be charging into a forest under normal circumstances, this one is completely encased in the academy grounds and the magical protections that are in place around it. Add in the fact it's crawling with members of the Huntsmen and various officers-in-training, and the chances of anything bad happening are slim to none.

"Help, help, arghhhhh," the person shouts.

I come to a stop as I notice a rope hanging between two trees with a sign on it saying not to go any further. The person's shouts are coming from further inside.

"Should we go get someone?" I ask Blanche.

She shakes her head. "They sound in a lot of pain, we should help first."

I nod, agreeing with her assessment. Our mother taught us everything she knows about dressing wounds and supporting injuries, and while that isn't as much as a proper healer, it's still plenty.

We duck under the rope. I keep my eyes peeled for anything dangerous, spying a couple of traps dotted around.

It must be something to do with the Huntsmen.

"Help!"

Hmm. There's something familiar about the voice, but that isn't too surprising. The academy isn't that big, I've probably met all of the students at one time or another.

I pass a big tree to find a figure writhing on the ground with their foot in a trap. I wave Blanche over and the two of us approach.

"Hello," I call. "We're here to help."

The figure looks up, revealing his face to us.

My eyes widen in surprise.

Hugo. What's he doing out here alone? And why did he ignore the signs warning him not to come into this part of the forest?

"What use are you going to be?" he demands.

I smile as sweetly as possible, but Blanche beats me to an answer.

"We've been helping animals out of traps since we were old enough to understand what they were," she says in a surprisingly cold tone. I didn't realise she'd spent enough time around Hugo to form an opinion of him.

"Well get on with it then."

I try not to roll my eyes.

Blanche crouches down by the trap and inspects it, while I search the nearby area for the right kind of leaves to make a temporary compress if he's bleeding badly.

"This is going to hurt for a moment, but then you'll be free," she warns him.

"Just do it," he insists sharply.

The grate of metal releasing cuts through the air. I wince, but manage to ignore it.

Hugo's scream of pain isn't so easily ignored.

He scrambles away from the trap. "What did you do that for?" he demands of Blanche.

She shoots me a confused look, but I shake my head. I have no idea what his problem is.

"I got you out." She points to the bloodied jaws of the trap. It doesn't look like he's cut himself too badly, but it's hard to tell from this angle.

"You hurt me," he whines.

Blanche huffs.

She's going to leave me, I can tell without even waiting for her to announce as much.

As if on cue, she storms off into the woods.

"Will you let me look at your ankle to make sure you haven't hurt yourself too badly?" I ask as calmly as possible. If I'm completely honest, I want to follow Blanche, but this is the right thing to do.

"No. Get away from me." Somehow, he manages to get to his feet, but he's very obviously unsteady.

"Please? It's better if..."

"I said no," he snaps.

"All right, then let me help you back to the castle," I suggest instead, still confused about why he doesn't want to make things easier on himself. I doubt it has anything to do with male pride.

"I don't want help. Especially not from you," he spits.

I frown. "What?"

"Everything is all your fault," he hisses at me.

I do a double-take. He isn't making much sense. Could he be delirious from the pain?

"My fault?" I squeak. "We helped you."

"If you weren't in the picture, that title would be all mine."

"What title? You mean Gavrel's?" So this isn't about me helping him at all? Why is he talking about this when there are clearly more important things happening?

"Who else am I going to mean?" he snaps. "Hardly yours."

I narrow my eyes. He shouldn't be talking to me like this, especially not when I helped him get out of the trap. Blanche had the right idea by storming off and leaving him to it. Perhaps I should have done the same.

"You're betrothed to Gavrel..."

Confusion washes through me at his accusation.

"I'm not," I cut him off. "It's none of your business, but if you're going to be awful to me about it then you should know I'm not betrothed to him at all, and that's not something Gavrel would ask me to do just to save his title. If you knew him at all, you'd know that."

His whole face turns bright red, right up to his ears. I doubt many of the girls at the academy would be calling him handsome now, though that's mostly down to his attitude rather than anything else. It isn't his fault he turns red when he's annoyed. But it is his fault that he can't control his anger.

I'm about to say something to that effect when he huffs and storms off in the direction of the castle, limping the entire way. He's moving much faster than someone in his predicament normally would. If I wasn't so confused, I might be impressed.

I stare after him, not quite understanding what just happened. Did he really just have a go at me after Blanche and I helped him out of the trap that could have destroyed his ankle if he'd continued the way he had?

I'll never understand some people. And definitely not him.

I sigh and begin the walk back to the castle alone. I should find Gavrel and tell him about what's happened. I'm sure he'll be able to offer some kind of explanation, especially with having known Hugo from before.

And, as much as I don't want to, I'm going to have to bring up what Hugo mentioned about a betrothal. I know it may be a touchy subject, but if it can help Gavrel avoid whatever it is Hugo is planning, then it's got to be worth exploring. It may still be early in our potential courtship, but I enjoy spending time with him. I can see how the two of us would work well together for a long time.

I push the thought aside. None of that matters until I've talked to Gavrel. I can't daydream about betrothals, weddings, and the future. We haven't even kissed yet.

Perhaps I should take matters into my own hands in that regard. Maybe I'll run it by Blanche, she's always been the more forward of the two of us. I wish she hadn't run off already or I could have talked to her about it now. Instead, I'm going to have to make the walk back up to the academy building with only my own thoughts for company.

Hopefully, my imagination doesn't run too wild on the way.

# CHAPTER 12

Gavrel passes me a full goblet of fruit wine. Our fingers brush as I take it from me, filling me with a giddy pleasure only being around him can bring me.

It's tempered somewhat by the meeting with Hugo in the woods. I know I need to talk to Gavrel about it, but there's a part of me that's reluctant to do it.

"What's wrong?" he asks me after I don't say anything for a while.

I take a deep breath. It's now or never.

"I saw Hugo in the woods," I start.

He sighs. "What did he do? If you need me to talk to him, then I can."

"I don't think he'd like that."

A wry chuckle escapes from him. "No, probably not."

"He was stuck in one of the animal traps the Huntsmen put out."

"No doubt he ignored all the warning signs about them."

"How did you know?" My surprise leeches through my voice.

"He's done it before. He's arrogant enough to often disregard anything that he should be listening to. It made him popular with the other students at Perault, but not with any of the teachers."

"Unsurprising."

"Very. I'm not sure why he thought it was a good idea to alienate the people in charge of him."

"Especially when he doesn't have a particularly impressive title."

"Indeed." Gavrel nods in agreement with my assessment. "So, what happened when you found him in the trap?"

"Blanche and I helped him out and then he was..." I trail off, unsure of exactly what words I'm looking for.

"Unreasonable?"

"Very. But he said something about me being to blame for him losing a chance at your title." I draw out the words, feeling unnecessarily awkward about them.

"Oh?"

"He said something about a betrothal."

Gavrel stiffens, telling me all I need to know about the potential truth in Hugo's words.

"He said that our betrothal would stop him from inheriting your title," I say, powering on when it becomes clear Gavrel isn't going to say anything.

"That's true," he admits. "There's a clause in the agreement that says if I'm betrothed before a certain point, then it won't happen."

"When is the point?"

"The start of the new year."

My eyes widen. "That's not even six months from now."

"I know. But my family is adamant that I don't give in to the pressure and force some girl to marry me because of this."

"But you don't have to marry her to be betrothed. You could end the arrangement once your title is secure."

"It doesn't work like that." Pain lances through his voice. "If I didn't marry the person I got betrothed to, Hugo would still get the title."

"Ah. So it's more than just a betrothal."

He nods.

"All right, then why don't we get betrothed?" The suggestion slips out before I've thought it through.

Except that isn't quite right. I've been thinking about the possibility ever since Hugo brought it up earlier.

"I know we haven't talked about it before. Or whether or not we're courting," I say quickly.

"We are," Gavrel cuts in.

Relief floods through me. At least I guessed that right. "Good. I thought so, but we didn't actually talk about it." I take a sip of wine, enjoying the sweet and tart flavours that explode on my tongue. I'm glad the academy lets the older students drink it. They're probably well aware that we all do at the formal functions in our home kingdoms. And with most dinners.

"I'm sorry, I should have thought to ask you formally."

I wave away his apology. "It's fine. I could have asked too, but didn't. And we're clearly both on the same page. But that brings me back to the betrothal..."

"I'm not getting betrothed to you," he says firmly.

"But..."

"No, Rose. I'm not trapping you into anything. It's not about how I feel about you now. Or how you feel about me. But can we guarantee we'll feel that way in six months? What about a year, or five? I can't do that to you when we've only known one another for a short period of time."

"But if it's the only way, surely it's worth the risk?" Despite my words, I actually do appreciate what he's saying, and I see the truth in them. I'm just not sure if it's worth losing his family's title over.

"It isn't the only way," he admits.

My eyebrows shoot up. "What is it?" I set my cup to the side.

"A duel."

"To the death?" Alarm fills me at the idea of him doing something so dangerous. I don't know anything about Hugo's duelling ability. Or Gavrel's for that matter, though I suspect he's got at least the very basic training needed given his knowledge of jousting and other sports.

"Just first blood."

Phew. That's not too bad. From what I've heard, first blood duels tend to be over quickly and not involve anything life-threatening. "Can you set one up?"

He shakes his head. "It's too risky. It could get me expelled from the academy at best. And I have a good reason to stay. I don't need a title to do well in life, especially with the education I'll get from this place."

"I suppose..." I trail off.

Gavrel reaches out and takes both of my hands in his. "I promise, Rose, it's not worth it. If you still want to keep courting me, then I have every-thing I need."

"You really think I'd want to stop just because you won't duel?"

He chuckles. "I was thinking more because I refused a betrothal offer."

"Oh." I hadn't thought about it like that. "But it's not a real refusal," I point out.

"In that it wasn't an official offer, yes. But I know how these things go..."

I lean forward to press a reassuring kiss against his cheek, but he moves at the last moment and my lips land on his.

Instead of pulling away, I lean into it.

Gavrel's hand cups my cheek as he kisses me back, and I'm very grateful the two of us are in a sheltered alcove in the castle gardens where no one can see us. This moment is one I want to treasure for a long time to come, I don't want it marred with an interruption.

He pulls away, staring at me intently. "I'm sorry, I didn't mean to do that."

"Neither did I," I assure him. "But I'm not sorry it did."

A low chuckle comes from him. "No, neither am I."

I beam, unable to contain my joy at what's growing between this. We may not have sorted out the problem named Hugo, but at least I now know what's happening between me and Gavrel. And for that, I'm grateful. For the former issue, I'll have to think of another way to help Gavrel keep his title. I don't want him to lose it because he wants to be a decent person, that isn't fair.

But I'm certain we'll come up with something. We have to.

CHAPTER 13

I burst into Blanche's room, hoping she's there with Joan. To be honest, I need her more than I need my sister right now.

"Rose!" Blanche cries. "What are you doing here?"

"I did something stupid," I blurt.

She closes her eyes and groans. "What?"

Joan sits quietly beside her, not saying anything. I suppose we don't know one another well enough for anything else.

I glance at my hands, unsure of the best way to broach the subject without sounding like a reckless fool.

"I may have sent Hugo Klein a note challenging him to a duel."

She blinks a few times, trying to process what I'm saying. "You did what?"

"I challenged Hugo to a duel," I repeat.

"Why?"

I launch into a long-winded explanation about Gavrel's title and needing to help him keep it. Both of them listen intently, not interrupting me at all. I'm grateful for that, it helps me get it all out.

"Is there any chance you can undo it?" Blanche asks.

I shake my head. "He already accepted." I hold up the piece of paper in my hand.

"And you want to know how to get out of it?" Blanche asks. "Right?" She gives me a look that says that better be the case.

I glance down at the ground. "Not exactly."

"What?" Blanche demands.

"She wants to know how to win," Joan says softly.

"You can't do this, you've never held a sword in your life." Blanche's voice is surprisingly high compared to normal.

"That's not true..."

"Fine. You've held a sword, but that doesn't mean you know what to do." She crosses her arms and glares at me as if I've done the most stupid thing in the world.

Perhaps I have. It was a spur of the moment decision that I'm starting to regret.

"Will you help me?" I ask Joan.

"Of course..."

"No, this isn't going to happen," Blanche counters, looking between the two of us with a stern expression on her face. "You can't help her do something this stupid."

"She's going to do it anyway," Joan points out. "If I don't help her, she could get really hurt."

Blanche purses her lips, probably seeing the truth of Joan's words but not wanting to admit it.

"I have a sword in my room." I had it delivered when I realised I was going to need one.

"Why can't you ask Gavrel to help?" Blanche asks.

"He doesn't know I'm doing this."

"But it's for him."

"Even more reason for him not to know. If he does, he'll stop it and he'll end up losing his title to Hugo. I can't let that happen."

Joan nods but Blanche continues to glare at me. She's not impressed. But I don't think I blame her. If the situation were reversed, then I might be as annoyed at her for being reckless.

"I have to do this. I think it'll help us put our prophecy to rest."

Blanche sighs loudly. "Fine. But I don't like it."

"I know. But I have to do this."

"I'll show you the basics," Joan promises. "What kind of duel is it?"

"To first blood."

"Good. That gives you more of a chance to win. You're going to have to focus on making sure it's over as quickly as possible. From everything I've heard about Hugo Klein, he'll have been trained to do this properly."

I nod.

She picks up two of the fireplace tools and hands one of them to me.

I take it, trying to get used to the weight of it. I haven't held the sword for very long, but it felt lighter than this. Hopefully, that'll make it easier.

"You're holding it wrong," Joan instructs. You need to make your wrist looser. If you hold the sword too tightly and he hits it, then you're going to end up with a wrist injury."

I nod, seeing what she means.

"May I?" she asks, gesturing to my hand.

"Of course." I don't want to ask her for help and then ignore her, especially if I want to win.

Joan reaches out and corrects the way I'm holding the poker. She moves onto my posture, making comments and suggestions to improve things.

I listen intently, putting as much of her advice into practice as possible. My nerves settle the more she tells me. There might even be a chance that I can win this. But as Joan says, it's going to be important that I end the duel as quickly as possible.

I'm not sure whether or not I have what it takes.

She helps me for another half an hour or so, pointing me in the right direction and making sure I don't do anything monumentally stupid.

"I'm sorry, I have class now," she says. "But I think you've got the basics. Just make sure you don't take any unnecessary risks, and try to finish it all as quickly as possible."

I nod. "Thank you, Joan. I appreciate it."

She smiles at me, seeming to genuinely have enjoyed herself. "You're welcome." She turns to Blanche and kisses her swiftly on the cheek. "I'll see you for dinner?"

"Of course." Blanche looks at her in a way I've never seen her look at anyone before. It's sweet beyond belief.

Joan slips out of the room and heads towards whatever class she has to get to.

I start to head towards the door myself.

"Sit down," Blanche instructs, a strict expression on her face.

My eyes widen. I don't think I've ever seen her like this. Apparently, today is a day of new expressions for my sister.

"Why are you doing something so reckless?" she asks.

"Would you do it for Joan?" I ask. "If a duel was the only way to save something that was important to her?"

Blanche sighs, and I know I've won her around. She understands exactly why I'm doing this, even if she doesn't want to admit it.

"So you and Gavrel..."

"We're officially courting," I admit, a wide grin on my face. "We kissed too."

She squeals in a very un-Blanche like way. She covers her mouth, almost as if she didn't expect to make the sound. "I'm sorry, that's just exciting."

"It is," I agree. "And you and Joan..."

She chuckles. "We've been courting for a while, you know that."

"I do. But is it going well?"

"I think so, but this isn't something I've done before."

"I know. It's new to me too. But at least the two of us are doing it together."

"Just the way twins should be," Blanche points out.

I reach out and take her hand in mine, giving it a squeeze. "I'm glad you have her. She seems like a lovely person."

"Thanks. And same with Gavrel. I like him."

"I'm glad. I wouldn't want to court someone who you don't like." While Blanche and I don't always see eye-to-eye, it's important to me that she likes the person I'm courting.

Things are looking good for the two of us, even if I do have a duel.

CHAPTER 14

The sword is heavier in my hand than I want it to be, but it's too late to do anything about that now. The duel is approaching and there's absolutely nothing I can do to change it. Forfeiting will leave us with the same problem we already have, and it's not going to protect Gavrel from losing his title.

Guilt wells up within me at the thought of keeping this from him still. Maybe I should have told him what I plan on doing, but I get the feeling he'd just have stopped me and that also won't help.

"Are you ready?" Hugo asks, a sneer on his face.

He thinks he's going to win.

Sadly, there's a part of me that fears that's true. But I'm trying not to dwell on it. If I think I'm going to lose, then there's no chance of me winning. I have to think like I'm going to.

"I'm ready."

"No seconds."

"It's only until first blood," I point out. "I don't think we need a second." And I'm not going to put anyone else in this situation. Technically, I'm not supposed to be duelling at all. Not only am I not trained, but the academy does technically ban students from taking part in them. I've been naively hoping that they treat it the same way they do a lot of other things and don't actually do anything to stop students who do get into the situation.

Hugo nods tersely and goes to take his spot opposite me.

I take a deep breath, trying to keep everything Joan has taught me over the past couple of days in my head. I was surprised when she showed up at my bedroom door the evening after she first helped me, but it turns out Blanche asked her if she wouldn't mind helping me more. I'm grateful for it.

Especially as she's standing to the side right now, acting as one of the witnesses. There's no point in doing something like this if there's no one here to corroborate the result. Hugo has brought one of his friends with him too. No doubt he doesn't trust mine. I don't blame him, I wouldn't trust him if the situations were reversed.

"When you're ready," Joan calls. "Begin."

I raise my sword and point it in Hugo's direction. I'm sure I'm not holding it right, but that's part of my plan. If he underestimates me, that's an advantage I can use.

He charges at me, I parry his blow, already feeling shaky.

I need to win this quickly. That's what Joan's been telling me this entire time. If this becomes a drawn-out fight, then I'm going to lose, I don't have the stamina or training to undo the damage he can cause.

I move forward, sticking my sword in Hugo's direction. It's probably not a recognisable manoeuvre, but that doesn't matter too much, so long as I manage to do what I came here for.

To my surprise, he jumps back in surprise. My blade slices along his hand, leaving a thin trail of blood behind it.

My eyes widen and I drop my sword down to my side.

Is that it?"

Hugo glances at the bright red streak across his hand, surprise and disbelief fighting for dominance on his face.

Joan steps forward, presumably to announce that the duel is at an end. But Hugo has another idea. He leaps forward, pointing his sword at me as he does.

I only just get mine up in time to block the attack.

"The duel is over," Joan half-shouts. "Put down your weapons."

Hugo comes at me again.

I stumble backwards, barely managing to keep a safe distance between us. I don't know what he thinks he's going to achieve by attacking me further, but he doesn't seem to have thought any of this through.

"No!" a familiar voice roars.

I turn my head in Gavrel's direction, shocked to see him standing there and staring at us with Blanche at his side. She doesn't look particularly impressed either.

Hugo takes advantage of my distraction and leaps forward, nicking my arm with his blade.

I yell out in pain and drop my sword on reflex.

Gavrel charges at Hugo, completely unarmed. He knocks him off his feet, causing his sword to spin in another direction. The two of them wrestle on the ground. I can't tear my eyes away in case Hugo does something foolish like pull out a dagger. Technically, he's not supposed to have had one according to duelling rules, but he's also supposed to stop once first blood has been reached, and he clearly didn't do that.

"Are you all right, Rose?" Blanche asks as she reaches me.

"I'm fine."

"Your arm..."

I glance down to find deep red staining the sleeve of my dress.

Oops. That's going to be a pain to fix.

"It's nothing," I assure her.

"Does it mean he won?" a thread of guilt comes through her question.

I shake my head. "I don't think so, I got him first."

She sighs with relief. "At least this hasn't been for nothing."

I hope she's right. There's a chance Hugo isn't going to accept the results of the duel, and if his friend is going to lie for him, then it'll be his word against ours. That's not going to end well.

A clatter draws my attention to the group of guards heading our way. I grimace. Someone must have realised what's happening and are coming to interfere.

I hope the others aren't going to get into too much trouble when this is my fault. Especially Gavrel. He didn't want to do this because of what it might mean for his time at Grimm Academy. I can't believe I've messed this up for him all while trying to fix the situation in the first place.

"What's going on here?" one of the guards asks. I don't know his name, mostly they keep to themselves and we never see any of the security team unless we leave the grounds.

His two comrades are already pulling Hugo and Gavrel apart.

I search for the best thing to say, but come up blank. Trying to explain the situation is just going to cause more problems.

"My sister is hurt," Blanche says instead, pointing to my sleeve. "She needs to go to the infirmary."

The guard frowns. "How did this happen?"

I glance at the ground. There's nothing on it. I have to come clean if I want any chance of saving my friends and sister from getting into trouble.

"I challenged Hugo to a duel," I admit.

The guard raises an eyebrow. "To first blood, I hope."

I nod. "But he didn't stop after I cut him."

He smothers a laugh, probably amused to think that I managed to one-up someone with training.

He sighs. "All right, let's get everyone to the infirmary to be checked out, but once that's cleared up, the headmistress will be wanting to see you."

I grimace. That's what I feared. But now we've been caught, there's nothing for it. I have to suffer the consequences, whether I want to or not.

CHAPTER 15

The atmosphere in the Headmistress' office is less than pleasant. I haven't spent any time here before, but I have to hope that it's not like this all the time. Most students who have been to see the Headmistress say nice things about her though, so I have to assume this isn't the norm.

"I didn't expect to see you in here, Rose," she says sternly.

"Even with my prophecy?" I attempt.

A small smile flits across her face, but she gets rid of it quickly enough. "You have a good point. I did expect to see you and your sister about your prophecy at some point. What I didn't expect was for you to be sitting here because you've been illegally duelling."

"In my defence, I never thought that would be the case either," I mutter.

"And yet you did it."

I sigh. "I had no choice."

"There's always a choice," the Headmistress reminds me.

"There wasn't one that I was comfortable with," I admit. "If I hadn't challenged Hugo to the duel, he would have stolen Gavrel's title." Oops, maybe I shouldn't have admitted to starting the whole situation myself. But it's not like Hugo won't have thrown me under the carriage for it already. He's not got anything to protect by keeping me blameless.

Quite the opposite. Though the fact he accepted my challenge probably doesn't look good.

"I can understand that." She taps on the cover of the big leather book sitting on her desk. "Do you know what this is?"

"The Grimm Academy rule book?" It's a guess, I actually have no idea, I've never even heard about the Headmistress having a big book in her office. To say she runs the entire academy, there's a surprising lack of gossip about her.

To my surprise, she chuckles. "That's not a bad guess, but no. This isn't the rule book. That's considerably bigger."

And probably includes a passage about what to do with students like me who break the rules. The worst bit being that I knowingly broke the rules. I didn't have to do it, but I did anyway.

"This is a book of prophecies. Every student who enters the academy with a prophecy hanging over their head is entered onto a page in the book."

My mouth hangs open. "Do our parents provide you with details?" I ask. Wouldn't they have told me about this?

"No. The book is a magical item. No one is completely sure how it works, but it does tell me when a prophecy has been completed or avoided."

Dread settles in the pit of my stomach. Is she about to tell me how badly my prophecy is going to turn out?

That doesn't seem likely, she'd have Blanche in here too if that was the case. I'm sure of it.

The Headmistress reaches for the book and opens it. She pushes it towards me so I can see the page she's directed me to.

The creamy page is covered in an elegant scrawl detailing all kinds of aspects of mine and Blanche's prophecy. But that's not what's caught my eye the most. I know the details, my parents have never tried to keep it from me, unlike some of the other students from the academy I know.

What catches my attention the most is the word avoided scrawled across the top of the page.

My eyes widen and relief floods through me.

"I'm not sure precisely how you made this happen," the Headmistress admits. "Of all the prophecies I've seen, yours is one of the vaguest I've witnessed. But this happened while you were taking part in your illegal duel."

"It worked?" Excitement rises within me. "Gavrel gets to keep his title?"

"Those are the terms of the contract between the two families," the Headmistress confirms. "If the contract was magically sealed, it will already be in force. If not, then I'm sure there are reports and witness statements that need to be submitted. But that is beside the point. We're not here to discuss Gavrel's situation, we're here to discuss yours."

Oh right. Somehow I forgot about that. I broke the academy rules and now I need to face the consequences.

"Hugo has been expelled from Grimm Academy," the Headmistress says. "He not only broke the rules by taking part in the duel, but he was helping another student's prophecy come true."

"What if he wasn't aware that's what he was doing? That doesn't seem fair." I'm not sure why I'm defending him, but it seems like the right thing to do.

"As far as I know, he wasn't aware. But we don't encourage the kind of behaviour he engaged in while here, especially when it endangered the welfare of one of our other students."

I suppose what he was doing to Gavrel was bad.

"Normally, when someone has had a hand in stopping someone else's prophecy, we award the student a scholarship to stay at the academy. However, in your case, you also broke the rules and that needs to be addressed."

I grab hold of my skirts and ball my hands into fists as I try to avoid showing my worry on my face.

"For that reason, and because you have a good academic record, we have decided that you won't be offered a scholarship, but you will be able to stay at Grimm Academy for the remainder of your studies."

My eyes widen. "I can stay?"

"Yes."

"But I didn't stop anyone's prophecy. Gavrel never said that's what he was dealing with..."

"Your sister was very clear about what she didn't do. Your prophecy was hers too and you are the one who suffered through the various stages of it."

"Oh." It sounds like they've made it up as an excuse to let me stay at the academy despite my rule-breaking. I'm not about to point that out, though. I'm going to stay very quiet and hope they forget about the whole thing.

"But please be aware that if you take part in any more duels or flout any other rules, you won't be given a reprieve a second time," she warns.

"Understood," I say quickly.

"In which case, you may go." She gestures towards the door.

"Thank you."

A smile spreads across the older woman's face. "You're very welcome."

I scamper out of the room, not wanting to linger too much in case the Headmistress changes her mind. I don't know if she has the power to do that, but I don't want to take the risk just in case.

I step outside to find Gavrel pacing back and forth nervously.

"Rose." He rushes forward and catches me in his arms. "Are you all right?"

I nod into his chest, returning his embrace as tightly as he's giving it to me. "And I get to stay here."

"You're not expelled?"

"No. But Hugo is."

"I know, they dragged him out of the grounds while he was shouting slurs at me."

"But he's gone?"

"Very gone."

I sigh with relief. "And your title?"

"Are you still worried about that?"

"I bled for that title."

He chuckles. "I suppose you did. The title is still mine and he won't ever get it."

Relief floods through me. "I'm glad."

"Did you really not like the idea of being with me if I didn't have a title?" he asks, a hint of hurt in his voice.

"I wouldn't have minded at all," I tell him honestly. "But I also didn't want you to lose anything because of me and not being betrothed."

"That's very sweet, but you shouldn't have put yourself in danger for me."

"It's done now. I promise not to do anything that reckless again."

"Why don't I believe you?"

Instead of answering, I go up on my toes and press a gentle kiss against his lips. He responds instantly, pulling me closer. I melt into him, enjoying everything about the moment.

I love the way he makes me feel, and on top of that, I'm now prophecy free.

EPILOGUE

ONE YEAR LATER

The setting sun illuminates the gardens, casting a warm orange glow all over the academy gardens and the music coming from one of the open windows only adds to the atmosphere.

Gavrel hands me a cup of wine.

Our fingers brush as I take it from him, sending welcome tingles through my whole body. He always makes me feel as if I'm the only person in his world.

"This is a rather elaborate picnic," I say, scanning over the multiple dishes he's managed to get the kitchens to produce.

"Is it? I hadn't noticed," he responds, but there's something off about his tone.

I raise an eyebrow. "I don't think we've ever had three types of pie in one go before. What did you tell the kitchens to get them to do this?"

"Nothing much, just that I wanted to make this evening special for you."

I frown, trying to think if there's anything special today. My birthday isn't for a couple of months and neither of us is nearing graduation. There's nothing special about today.

I take a sip of my wine, the delicious taste of it hitting my tongue. "You got my favourite wine."

"Yes." He continues setting things out on the picnic blanket in front of us.

A flaky pastry with almonds on top joins the rest of the food.

"And my favourite desserts...I'm starting to get a little suspicious. Are you trying to end our courtship?"

Shock crosses Gavrel's face. "Why would I get all of your favourite things if I wanted to end things?"

"I have no idea, maybe to soften the blow? I've not been in this situation before."

"I don't think you've been in this one either," he jokes.

"I won't be able to confirm that until you tell me what you're up to," I point out.

Gavrel sighs. "I know, I'm just trying to set the mood."

Confusion rushes through me. "You're going to have to make things clearer."

"I'm sorry, I'm nervous."

I set my cup down on the blanket and reach out for his hands. I take them in mine and meet his gaze.

He's not lying about the nerves, I can see them in the way his eyes shift around my face as he tries to determine how I'm responding to all of this.

"I'm not sure what this is about, but I can assure you it's going to be fine. We've already managed to stop my prophecy and kept your title in the process," I point out.

He chuckles. "I suppose that is true. But somehow, this feels even more serious than either of those things."

"I'll admit I'm intrigued."

Gavrel takes a deep breath. "Do you remember that talk we had about being betrothed?"

"Vaguely. It's been a while."

Where is he going with this? I wish I could tell, but it's hard to read without more information.

"I'd like to revisit it."

"The conversation?"

"Yes."

"Didn't you tell me that you didn't want to get betrothed during it?" I ask.

"I did, but that's the bit I want to revisit."

"Oh." Is he trying to remind me that he doesn't want things to be serious with me anymore?

"I want to start talking to my father about starting the betrothal formalities. But I know that will involve reaching out to your family and I want to make sure you're on board with the process. I guess I'm asking if you want this or not. If you say no, I won't talk to my father about it."

"And if I say yes?"

"Then I'll send the letter that's been sitting on my desk for several months."

"Oh." It takes a moment for what he's saying to sink in. "Are you asking me whether I want to marry you?"

"Yes. Not right away, I'm asking for a long betrothal to give us a chance to finish our education and to get ourselves settled."

"That's so thoughtful." I know a lot of women back home who talk about how much they regret not having time like I've had.

"There'll obviously be a clause in the contract so you can break it if you want."

"I hope it will say that you can do that too." I don't want him to be trapped any more than I want myself to be either.

"Of course. We'll future proof it," he promises.

"Then send the letter."

"Are you sure?"

"More sure than I've been about anything. I did risk my life for you," I point out.

A soft snort escapes him. "It was a duel to first blood."

"Try telling Hugo that," I mutter.

"True."

I reach out and cup his cheek in my hand. "But I'll gladly start the betrothal process with you."

He smiles broadly, clearly pleased with my answer.

I lean in and press my lips against his. I shuffle closer so I can deepen the kiss.

A content glow floods through me at his touch and at the thought of what's to come for the two of us. It's so sweet of him to ask before he starts the process. A lot of people wouldn't think to do that.

I have no qualms about saying yes. Or telling my family I want to when the time comes. There's a peace to the decision, and I'm sure that means it's the right one.

And that we have a great future in front of us.

***

Thank you for reading *Roses Of Regret*, I hope you enjoyed it! If you want to continue the series, you can with *Princess Of Petals*, a Beauty and the Beast retelling.

AUTHOR NOTE

Thank you for reading Roses Of Regret, I hope you enjoyed it!

If you're familiar with the original tale, you may have noticed that I've switched the personalities of the sisters. Rose Red is normally the outspoken one, whereas in Roses Of Regret it is Blanche (Snow White) who is more that way. The main reason for this was that I got mixed up on which was which while writing Glints Of Gold, and gave Rose the calmer of the two personalities. I could have gone in and changed the names over, but decided against it as I thought the story being told from the quieter of the two sisters' points of view would be more interesting. Rose was also the natural protagonist for Roses Of Regret for a couple of reasons - the first being the title (which was actually the first title in the Once Upon An Academy series that I had), and the other was to minimise confusion between this version of Snow White, and the Snow White who appears in Mirrors and Magic. That is also why Blanche is called Blanche and not Snow, a departure from how I normally name the characters in the Grimm World. (Though not if you understand French!)

For those of you who know German names, you may have noticed that Klien is a German surname for small in reference to the dwarf from the original tale of Snow White and Rose Red.

If you haven't read the twins' friend Zerrin's story, then you can in book 3 of the Once Upon An Academy series, Glints Of Gold.

If you want to keep up to date with new releases and other news, you can join my Facebook Reader Group or mailing list.

Stay safe & happy reading!

\- Laura

Also By Laura Greenwood

Signed Paperback & Merchandise:

You can find signed paperbacks, hardcovers, and merchandise based on my series (including stickers, magnets, face masks, and more!) via my website.

Series List:

* denotes a completed series

The Obscure World

A paranormal & urban fantasy world where supernaturals live out in the open alongside humans. Each series can be read on its own, but there are cameos from past characters and mentions of previous events.

<u>Cauldron Coffee Shop</u> - <u>Broomstick Bakery</u> - <u>Obscure Academy</u> - <u>The Shifter Season</u> - <u>Grimalkin Academy</u>* - <u>City Of Blood</u>* - <u>Grimalkin Vampires</u>* - <u>Supernatural Retrieval Agency</u>* - <u>The Black Fan</u>* - <u>Sabre Woods Academy</u>* - <u>Scythe Grove Academy</u>* – <u>Ashryn Barker</u>*

The Forgotten Gods World

A fantasy romance world based on Egyptian mythology.

<u>Forgotten God</u>

The Egyptian Empire

A modern fantasy world set in an alternative timeline where the Egyptian Empire never fell.

<u>The Apprentice Of Anubis</u>

The Paranormal Council Universe

A paranormal romance & urban fantasy world where paranormals are hidden away from the human world, and are in search of their fated mates. Each series can be read on its own, but there are cameos from past characters and mentions of previous events.

<u>The Paranormal Council Series</u>* - <u>The Fae of the Paranormal Council Universe</u>* - <u>Paranormal Criminal Investigations</u>* - <u>The Necromancer Council</u>*

Other Series

<u>Purple Oasis</u> (with Arizona Tape) - <u>Grimm Academy</u> - <u>Beyond The Curse</u>* - <u>Untold Tales</u>* - <u>The Dragon Duels</u>* - <u>Speed Dating With The</u>

<u>Denizens Of The Underworld</u> (shared world) - <u>Seven Wardens</u>* (with Skye MacKinnon) - <u>Tales Of Clan Robbins</u> (co-written with L.A. Boruff) - <u>Firehouse Witches</u>* (with Lacey Carter Andersen & L.A. Boruff) - <u>Mountain Shifters</u>* (with Lainie Anderson)

Twin Souls Universe

A paranormal romance & urban fantasy world co-written with Arizona Tape. Each series can be read on its own, but there are cameos from past characters and mentions of previous events.

<u>Amethyst's Wand Shop Mysteries</u> - <u>Twin Souls</u>* - <u>The Vampire Detective</u>*

About Laura Greenwood

Laura is a USA Today Bestselling Author of paranormal, fantasy, urban fantasy, and contemporary romance. When she's not writing, she drinks a lot of tea, tries to resist French macarons, and works towards a diploma in Egyptology. She lives in the UK, where most of her books are set. Laura specialises in quick reads, whether you're looking for a swoonworthy romance for the bath, or an action-packed adventure for your latest journey, you'll find the perfect match amongst her books!

Follow Laura Greenwood

Website: www.authorlauragreenwood.co.uk

Mailing List: https://www.authorlauragreenwood.co.uk/p/book-sign-up.html

Facebook Group: http://facebook.com/groups/theparanormalcouncil

Facebook Page: http://facebook.com/authorlauragreenwood

Bookbub: www.bookbub.com/authors/laura-greenwood